Better Homes and Gardens®

There's a Monster In My Soup

Ozzy stared at his steaming bowl of
alphabet soup. It didn't taste quite right. He
picked up the star-covered green can.

"Hmmm. This isn't the kind Mom usually
buys," Ozzy told Max, who was staying for
lunch.

"Mine is too hot to eat!" said Max.

"Maybe I left it on the stove too long,"
Ozzy said. As he picked up his spoon, the
soup started to gurgle and bubble. Letters
floated to the surface. Ozzy sounded them
out.

"D-R-O-O-G-L-E. What's a Droogle?" he
said as a tomato-colored cloud rose from his
soup bowl. It hovered over the table. "Yikes!"
gasped Ozzy, and he quickly backed away.

"There's a m-m-m-monster sitting in the middle of the table," Ozzy stammered.

"No way!" said Max. But when the wispy cloud disappeared, there was indeed a monster.

"Who are you?" said Ozzy.

"Droogle," said the sharp-toothed creature.

"Where did you come from?" asked Max. But before the monster could answer, Ozzy's soup began to bubble again. More letters floated to the top.

"Gleezit," read Ozzy.

"Klugger and Zoot," read Max.

The entire kitchen was filled with three more tomato-colored clouds. Then there were three more monsters on the table! They already had squished the jelly sandwiches and spilled the soup.

"What do you want?" asked Ozzy.

"Lunch," said Droogle. "We're hungry!"

The other monsters nodded and growled—all except Zoot, who was the smallest. "I want to go home," he cried.

"Ozzy, you'd better get them something to eat," said Max.

"Yeah," agreed Ozzy, and he scurried about the kitchen grabbing at everything. He took bananas, crackers, and corn whizzers from the cupboard. Max took milk, pickles, and apples from the refrigerator. He sped back to the table.

The hungry monsters made a grab for the food. Ozzy stepped back, a bit startled. "Stop that!" he said. "Sit down first!"

Zoot began to cry. But the other monsters didn't notice as they jumped off the table and scrambled for the chairs. Zoot was knocked to the floor, and Max quickly rescued him from being squashed.

Max put the small monster in a baby's high chair. Then he and Ozzy quickly put all the food on the table.

The bigger monsters dived at it. They gulped and grabbed at the food. Poor little Zoot got nothing. And he hooted and hollered until Max made him a jelly sandwich all his own.

When the food was gone, the monsters began to bang the table with their fists. "Agggh! We want more!" shouted Klugger.

"There's nothing left," Ozzy whispered to Max. "We've got to get them out of the house. Mom doesn't even like *hamsters!*"

"We've still got the bag of corn whizzers," Max said. "I have an idea." He handed the bag to Ozzy. "Scatter these on the floor and head for the door."

Ozzy did, and the monsters followed
behind him, scooping up the corn whizzers
as they waddled out of the kitchen.
    But little Zoot was left in the high chair
and once more let out a frightful yowl.

Max carried Zoot to the backyard. "Maybe
we could play a game," he said as he tried to
put the baby monster down. But Zoot clung
tightly to Max's shirt.

Ozzy rolled his eyes to the sky. "Oh, sure!"
said Ozzy. "I can just see us playing hide-
and-go-seek with monsters."

But Droogle jumped up and down. And
Klugger wiggled his little pointed ears and
clapped his paws. "Hide-and-seek!" yelled
Gleezit.

"You're it," shrieked Droogle, pointing at
Max.

Ozzy looked helplessly at Max as he and
the monsters scattered throughout the yard.
Max and Zoot leaned against the tree and
began to count.

"Ready or not, here I come," Max yelled. He turned around and pretended to look for the hiding monsters. He could see tails sticking out from behind trees and horns poking up through bushes.

But Max ignored them all and only looked in places that were too small for big monsters to hide. "There must be a way to make monsters disappear," Max thought.

Zoot whimpered. "I want to go home."

Max wiped away the small monster's tears. "I'll do my best," he said. "But how can I send you back? You're here by magic. I guess you'll have to disappear the same way."

Then he remembered the strange, star-covered green soup can Ozzy had been holding, and he ran for the kitchen.

Once inside, Max put Zoot in the high
chair. Then he found the can under the
kitchen table.

Max read the label, *"WARNING—DO NOT
OVERCOOK!* In case of an *emergency*, cross
your arms and repeat these words:

> Zim, Zam, Zowie.
> Pit, Putt, Powie.
> Wugger Worm
> Wugger Worm
> Skrit, Scrat, Scram."

Max looked out the door. He saw Ozzy's
mother coming back from the neighbor's
with a big plate of cookies.

As Ozzy's mother walked past the hiding
monsters, they followed her, one by one.

"Oops!" said Max. "They must be hungry
again! If this isn't an *emergency*, I don't
know what is!" And he crossed his arms and
said the silly words.

When he peeked out the door once more,
the monsters were gone. Only Ozzy, his
mother, and three tomato-colored clouds
were there. Then Max remembered Zoot.
He looked around the kitchen.

A little cloud hung over the high chair.
And in the middle, Max could see a small,
smiling monster. Max waved good-bye.

Zoot waved back. His smile lingered for a
moment, then he, too, was gone.

"Oh, no! What a mess you boys make when you cook," said Ozzy's mother as she came through the door. "And what do I smell?"

Max stared at Ozzy, who had followed her into the kitchen. "Uh . . . I think we overcooked the soup," said Max.

Ozzy's mother looked at the empty soup can. "This isn't the kind I usually buy," she said. "But they had a big sale. I have *five* more cans."

Monster Suit

Wear a paper-bag costume and pretend you're a scary monster.

What you'll need...

- Scissors
- 1 brown paper bag
- 1 crayon or pencil
- Monster Fur (see page 32)

1 For the arms, cut a slit about 10 inches long up the center of one narrow side of the bag. At the end of the slit, cut to the right and to the left just to the fold of the bag. This makes a T shape (see photo). Repeat on the other side of the paper bag.

2 Put the paper bag over your head. Have an adult use a crayon to mark the eye holes on the paper bag. Remove the bag from your head. Cut out the holes for your eyes (see photo).

3 Make a face on the monster any way you like. Then, decorate the body with Monster Fur (see photo and page 32).

Silly Monster Faces

Draw a funny monster face on the shape of your hand.

28

What you'll need...

- Newspaper or brown kraft paper
- 1 paper towel
- 1 plastic-foam meat tray or plate
- Water
- Tempera paint
- Construction paper
- Markers or crayons
- White crafts glue
- Glitter

1 Cover your work surface with newspaper. Fold a paper towel so it fits into the meat tray. Dampen the paper towel with water and place it in the tray. Pour a little paint over the paper towel. Press your hand into the paint. Then press your hand onto the construction paper (see photo). Let the picture dry.

2 Make a face on the monster any way you like.
   If you want to, draw hands and feet on the monster with markers. Decorate the monster by sprinkling lines of glue with glitter (see photo). Remove the excess glitter and save for another use.

Stick Monsters

Use your monster pals to put on a puppet show.

What you'll need...

- 1 paper nut cup or egg carton cup
- White crafts glue
- 2 wiggle eyes or buttons
- 1 small cork
- Creature Features (see page 32)
- Yarn
- Tape
- 1 crafts stick, straw, or unsharpened pencil

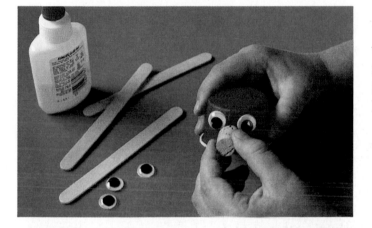

1 Turn the nut cup upside down. For the eyes, glue the wiggle eyes to the cup. For the nose, glue the cork to the cup (see photo). Also, see Creature Features on page 32.

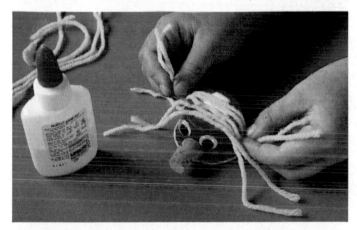

2 For the hair, cut several pieces of yarn about 5 inches long. Spread some glue on top of the nut cup. Lay the center of the pieces of yarn side by side in the glue (see photo). Let the glue dry.

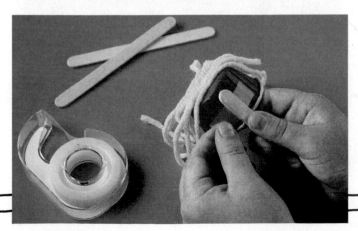

3 Tape a crafts stick to the back of the nut cup on the outside or inside (see photo).

Monster Suit

Decorate your monster with some of these "fuzzy" ideas.

Monster Fur: For paper fur, try this. Cut a square or rectangle from construction paper. Then, cut a thin strip of paper from one end *almost* to the other end, leaving about 1 inch at the top uncut. Repeat this until the whole piece of paper is cut into strips. Wrinkle the paper. Put glue on the uncut part of the paper fur. Stick it onto the monster body.

You can color fur on your monster with crayons and markers. And, you can glue things such as dried beans or peas, cotton balls, or strips of crepe paper or curling ribbon on the monster to make it look furry.

Maybe you can think of a funny rhyme or poem about your monster. Here's one:

There once was a monster
  from Yonder,
Who, every Wednesday, did
  wander,
Through forest and trees.
(He once found some bees.)
And now he is fonder of
  Yonder.

Silly Monster Faces

Besides your hand, can you think of other shapes that would make neat monsters? A leaf, a stick, or a funny-shaped rock? Or, your foot or shoe? Use a pencil to trace around the shape the same way you did with your hand.

You can make a puzzle out of your monster picture, too. After it's decorated, cut the picture into four or five pieces. Then mix up all the pieces and put them back together.

Stick Monsters

Make a happy-faced monster. Or, a scary or sleepy one. Pick ideas from this list or make up your own.

Creature Features: Use buttons, beads, dried pasta and macaroni, or gummed paper hole reinforcements for the monster's face. Tissue paper, wrapping paper, construction paper, felt, pipe cleaners, ribbon, toothpicks, cotton balls, and corks work, too.

You can build a hiding place for your Stick Monster out of a medium or large paper or plastic cup. Just follow these steps.

● Pick a paper cup big enough for the monster's head to fit in.
● Have an adult cut a small hole in the bottom of the cup big enough for the crafts stick to fit through.
● From the inside of the cup, push the crafts stick through the hole.
● Hold the cup in one hand. With the other hand, hold the crafts stick and push the monster in and out of his hiding place.

BETTER HOMES AND GARDENS® BOOKS

Editor: Gerald M. Knox   Art Director: Ernest Shelton   Managing Editor: David A. Kirchner
Department Head, Family Life: Sharyl Heiken

THERE'S A MONSTER IN MY SOUP

Editors: Jennifer Darling and Sandra Granseth   Graphic Designers: Brenda Lesch and Linda Vermie
Editorial Project Manager: Angela K. Renkoski
Contributing Writer: Nancy Buss   Contributing Illustrator: Buck Jones
Contributing Color Artist: Sue Fitzpatrick Cornelison   Contributing Photographer: Scott Little

Have BETTER HOMES AND GARDENS® magazine delivered to your door.
For information, write to: ROBERT AUSTIN, P.O. BOX 4536, DES MOINES, IA 50336